Memorial Day

Also by John Ratti

A REMEMBERED DARKNESS

MEMORIAL DAY

Poems by

JOHN RATTI

The Viking Press

New York

A number of the poems in this book have appeared
previously in issues of *New Directions* anthology,
Salmagundi, and *Hanging Loose*.

For Richard Tedeschi

. . . The woman startled and pulled away too quickly out of herself, too violently, so that her face remained in her two hands. I could see it lying in them, its hollow form. It cost me indescribable effort to stay with those hands and not to look at what had torn itself out of them. I shuddered to see a face from the inside, but still I was much more afraid of the naked flayed head without a face.

—From Rainer Maria Rilke,
The Notebooks of Malte Laurids Brigge
(Translated by M. D. Herter Norton)

CONTENTS

Memorial Day

RED TULIPS

It is the scratch of the dry black-tipped
    stamens
that opens the tulips to the light;
it is the cold red gasp of their petals
that closes them again.
The tight green buds became this;
the soft red flesh cannot go back.

FALLING

for R.T.

"*Amid all the beauty and splendour
of Peterborough cathedral, the thing
which intrigued me most was the
12th-century carving at the base of a
pillar . . . of a man tormented by
devils . . . the headlong fall of
Simon Magus, the magician, who
attempted to fly from the top of a
building. High above him . . . stands
the serene figure of St. Peter. . . .*"
(*from a letter to the editor of*
Country Life)

Let there be no mistake:
I am Simon Magus,
curly haired and wild-eyed,
brought to earth;
tormented living
by Christ's harsh wood
and rusty nails,
tormented
as I fall,
dying,
by live demons,
succubi of pain,
who make my headlong
plunge
continue

after I have ceased
to fall,
who tear at me
endlessly,
giving me an immortality
of pain.
For the more they take,
the more I am;
Heaven reconstitutes me
for Hell's pleasure,
shuttlecock
in the loveplay
of God and Devil.
Divinely titillated,
Prince Lucifer
spends himself
in my open wounds,
flashing his arrogant
teeth in steely
satisfaction.
From a parapet,
from a tower,
I tried to fly
beyond them all,
telling my words and spells
from my lips,
making a web
of threadlike
incantations

only
to have it cut,
at the instant of escape,
by the knife of
divine reason,
and I fall
trying to hold up
my sinking stomach
with my hands.
Triumphant and serene,
Saint Peter
weathers on a gable,
his eyes eaten out
by the wind.
And I,
eternally
reaching
bottom,
retain the full
definition
of my pain,
each stroke
of the master-carver
still cut deep
and true.

JOURNEY

detail from The Journey of the Magi
by Benozzo Gozzoli (1420–1497).

It is not God incarnate
whom they see,
these regal adolescents,
as they pause, reflective,
in their journey.
The faces of the pages
are too beautiful
for piety:
gilded with light
the color of fine honey;
the skin drawn too tight
for innocence
across their perfect cheekbones
by the knotted tension
in the painter's hand.
Secret onanists,
each of them,
Lorenzo the Magnificent
as a stripling Magus
included.
At first glance,
their eyes seem mild enough,
well-mannered,
inclined to roll
discreetly
into space.

On closer inspection
it becomes apparent
that their thoughts
are gathered, tumescent,
beneath their doublets,
separate and yet together,
the journey out
become the journey in.
Their downright Hellenistic legs,
frozen in midstep,
are skinned with cerise,
rust, blue, and olive hose,
which bags slightly,
and for all time,
in the sweaty hollows
behind their knees.

AS IT IS

at Hampton Court

The palace spells
its own name;
a fact not
buildings;
an artificial
headache world
taken root;
the maze,
a bad old joke
that's kept
its secret
punchline
coiled lethal
at its heart;
the gardens
that cram
the asking
mouth
with flowers
and answer,
curving in upon
themselves,
nothing;
the rectangular
fish ponds,
cataracted
blind
with yellow water
and enclosed

9

by ancient
trees.
English boys,
arranged neatly
in the perfect
intervals
between the trees,
cast their elegant
barbed lines
onto the water,
creels ready
but empty
still.

In the park
sheep graze
down the grass;
a sick ewe
slumps against
a tree
for comfort;
the others
hover near
but do not
approach
the pain
directly;
the deer,
not

quite tame,
move beyond
the flock
and run suddenly,
hooves
whistling
through the grass,
the speed
imagined
in their
delicate skulls
blossomed
in their antlers.
Lying in the grass,
you sleep.
The sun here
is old
and polished;
your hand
uncurls
to the warmth,
palm up:
the question;
the answer;
all I can
or will
know.

SERMON ON HUMAN PROGRESS

Hans Christian Andersen
told the tale
of a girl who danced
with bleeding feet,
exquisite pain,
and endless grace
on knife points.
An order of nuns
in New Jersey
still makes
hair shirts
and other barbed
appliances to order,
their price
(calculated
on the amount
and quality
of pain provided)
allows the sisters
beer
in the convent garden
on Saturday nights.
I know
a man
who likes
his taut white thighs
and sandy pubic hair
so much
that he wears

a leather strap
lined with spikes
around the base
of his penis
when he makes love.
What did you do
today
to help humanity
on its way
to ultimate satisfaction?
I think I'll
thrust
a wasp's nest
down the tender
waiting gullet
of the world
and let it go
at that.

RECURRENT DREAM

after Francis Bacon

I dreamed of you
in that recurrent dream
where
a lily-scented
three day corpse
is laid out
in a jewel box coffin
in the other room,
a horror just beyond the door,
half, quarter seen.
In all this time
I had forgotten
the white parts
of your body
and their dark words,
risen bubbling
on your lips.
Now it returns
at the moment
when
we were flayed
alive and screaming
on your rumpled bed,
skinned down
to our teeth and skulls.
And your pleasure of me
and my tearing hunger
spawned the horror
in the room
beyond the door.

TRIPTYCH

for Richard Kathmann

1

Twisting, turning

The black apple tree
twists from the earth
with the tense,
searching gesture
of a hand
pivoting on the wrist
as far as it will go
and freezing,
fingers, branches splayed
by the tension
of the turn,
fingers choked
with the fact
of bone beneath the skin,
branches rasped
tightly into place
by the granite sockets
of their deep roots.
And the fruit of the turning:
the scarlet apples of fall
have gone to bronze
in the freezing cold,
puckering the memory
of their living scream

into the folds
of dry, brittle skin;
the fingers,
transfixed with the tension
of their swollen gristle,
bud into thin air,
ready to burst
against the sweetness
of the silent flesh.

2

Full front

Fools of God,
the monks work
in the fields,
and in the woods
where they have
tacked their icons
to the tree trunks.
Their arms are bared,
their robes hitched up
and knotted at the waist.
The water clear
noon sun
washes across

their bearded mouths
and love whirled eyes.
Two monks
truss a pig up
to a young birch tree
with wire,
slit the squeal
from his throat,
and with a downward stroke
let his belly out
onto the grass.
They smile,
bless themselves,
and brush the flies
from their strong,
blood-spattered legs.
Then they cut the wire
and lug
the tepid carcass home.

3

And to turn again

"I come from Barre,
Barre, Barre, Barre,
over there—

call my sister
in Barre,
tell her to come."
The boy stood
in the play yard,
feet planted
in the gravel,
not moving them
but twisting,
turning his body
toward the mountains
by pivoting on his ankles,
moving the slits
of his black cat eyes,
sliding them
toward the mountains.
"Barre, Barre, Barre,
over there."
Thin white shirt
in the wind.
Straight Indian hair.
His skull
is too small
for his brain,
his brain too big
for his mind,
his mind wanting
to cross the mountains
to his kin,

but rooted
to the ground,
dug in.
"Call my sister,
call my sister
in Barre, Barre, Barre."
His pants
are too small
for his short, thick legs,
his sex too big
for his pants,
his mouth
frozen to an O
of wanting
to be heard,
to be told of
"in
Barre, in Barre,
in Barre."

"IN SURE AND CERTAIN HOPE..."

Arrogant, hips cocked,
bronze Saint John-the-Baptist-
as-a-boy,
brandishing a cross,
rides the stone pinnacle
of a Victorian
funerary monument,
poised above the sad
cocoons of bone and cloth
lying,
after worms,
beneath.
Baptized into hope,
they lived and died,
were placated for a while
with peach and yellow
gladioli
and beaded wreaths
and were forgotten.
Now they lie
in flesh rich soil
and dream the time
when they will rise
as holy butterflies
from their shroud-wrapped
grubs,
to fly beyond
the time-greened curls
and reedy cross.

THE MASTER'S EYE

Eakins' photograph of Bill Duckett

Reclining,
young Duckett
rests his weight
on his right arm,
his long legs
stretched out,
the right straight,
the left cocked up,
opening his body
to the master's
wide glass eye.
Whether or not
excitement
at being seen
has weighted
his penis
a bit
so that it falls
a little heavily
to the right
against his belly
is academic.
It is,
in fact,
the angle of his head
bowed in shadow,
the honest tension
in his right shoulder
and upper arm,

the slim
relaxed hand,
the perfect testicles
fallen against
his right leg
that explain
the fierce tenderness
in the master's
lidless eye.

WIND BELL

The triangle of weathered copper
suspended by a green iron hook
from the tip of the tongue of the wind bell
that hangs from a branch
of the tree in the garden
moves delicately as a razor blade
on a string,
one way, then another, then back,
but not far enough to ring the bell
or scare away the winter birds
who perch around it,
made fearless by hunger
and the cold.

TOURISTS

for Mary Lee Settle

1   (*Binsey*)

The water in the holy well
is ice cold
and dark;
there are no pilgrimages
across the meadow
from Oxford now;
the vicar's grass
conceals
the stone steps down.
Inside,
Saint Margaret's church
is silver tan,
the color of dust,
and the dark splotched
legends
of sainthood
and of Nicholas Breakspear
are scrubbed out
to the same
dust color,
no darker,
no brighter.

2   (*The Tower of London*)

The chapel of the hellhole
Tower
is silent
and sanded clean,
wood smooth,
floors scrubbed,
the black thunder
of monumental screams
torn from famous
mouths,
the eviscerated
scarlet shriek
into eternity
whispers
only softly
in the rafters,
no more
no less
insistent
than the sound
of pigeons
outside.

3 (*The Little Cloister,*
Westminster Abbey)

The ancient sound,
as perfect
as potent
as cruel
a charm
as a dried heart
pierced by dry thorns,
of water
falling
drop by drop
from a stone fountainhead
into a stone basin
is all
that holds
these stones
one upon
another.

STAY WITH ME
I AM ALONE

King Ludwig to his brother Otto

Come Otzi—
I will take you with me
in the sleigh tonight.
The lanterns are
flaming wolves' teeth
as they bite
the black flesh
of the night,
as they snap
at the dark pine boughs.
The horses
smoke as they run,
hot muscles stretched
against the cold.
Otzi, I have promised
Christ and the Liebfrau
that I'll stop.
But for you—
we'll go to the forester's
little house, and the men
will dance naked for us
by the fire,
and the fleshy buds
of our desire
will burst open
in the heat and smoke,
you'll see.

And when we all are drunk,
we will touch them—
Otzi, do you hear me?
If you stay with me,
I would do all this for you.
My crimes
gall Christ's wounds;
they tear
the Liebfrau's tender breasts.
I kiss your wild eyes,
Otzi—
my flesh
touching your flesh
brings our flesh
together.

PASSAGE

The fields of late summer
open their flatness
to the shuddering
cleaver falls of birds,
the absolute, deadly accuracy
of their downward stroke
creasing at one blow
the ribbed order
of the dying grass.

The deaf-mute boys
sealed
in the yellow tube
of their bus
cross the fields,
signing their brags,
whispering their fingers,
laughing little grunts
deep inside
their virgin throats.
In the empty, curving bell
of their silence,
beyond the swagger
of their hands,
they lock onto
each other
with their eyes
and speak out
with one voice.

The birds rise
straight up,
suddenly releasing the fields,
healing them with their absence.
They fix on distance
and,
in a straight black line,
enter it.

The bus disappears
separately,
the road emptied,
drawn taut between
gone and going.

GENEALOGY

for my father

When my many times
great-grandfather
deserted
Napoleon's army,
he made for
the Crimea,
had himself
headed up
in a barrel
and smuggled aboard
an Italian ship
bound for Gibraltar.
A friendly sailor
from Genoa
fed him
through the bunghole
until the ship
was far at sea.
When he got home
at last
to Pietrasanta
he stayed there.
His daughter
at a hundred
remembered
three things:
his return,
how to stanch
the flow of blood

with a cobweb,
and the way
they gathered seasalt
from hollows
in the rocks
along the shore.
My own grandfather
filled his deep
earth-floored cellar
with wine
made from his grapes,
and gathered snails
in the wet grass
of the garden
for pickling
in a wooden nail keg.
He kissed
the corner of his house
when he left
and when he returned.
There is a field
in Vermont
where I began
and where I end.

Moving her hands,
tilting her head
(heavy tulip blossom
on a neck gone fragile
as a stem),
swaying in her chair
from a still tight waist,
she showed me how
she had danced
the clean, black, fugal
lines of Bach
forty years before.
All her fury
at the untidiness
of years, disease, and dying
concentrated
in the steel grace
of her thin hands,
taut and hissing bowstring neck,
and coiled trunk.
Fearing softness,
she called
lustful women
"unclean";
when she saw Canova's
buttery, penis-centered
Perseus
she said, out loud,
"Who the hell

do you think
you are?"
She studied sea creatures,
marveling at crabs,
miming coral pinnacles
with her hands and trunk,
admiring
their perfect adaptation
to their world.
When she died,
her will commanded
that her ashes
be thrown into the sea.

COLLAPSE OF THE BROADWAY CENTRAL HOTEL

1973

England's golden Rupert,
dead almost sixty years now,
stayed here,
made fun of the Yanks,
and escaped to Staten Island
when the noise of the horsecars
and the democratic mob
of lower Broadway
became too wearing.
Part of the hotel collapsed
last week,
a pet dog was saved
from the rubble,
an old man or two
failed to escape,
and for several days
the surprised, empty rooms
gawped at the street,
rose wallpaper, washbasins
and all.
Rupert's lyrics
and fervent night sweats
are almost forgotten,
but the image
of him hanging
by his heels,

naked,
from the limb of a tree near Grantchester,
talking all the while,
remains.

TUMESCENT LUCIFER

Tumescent Lucifer
is a good old boy,
well pleased to offer
us the tickly joy
of his hot shaft rising
sharply upward from the burning
hells-nest of his balls;
sprawled on his locker-room throne,
still damp from the Stygian shower stalls,
grinning at the clench-toothed groan
of pleasure
he gives us—at his leisure,
not having to assist
the great erection up
with his horny fist,
just sitting, knowingly
enjoying us enjoying him—eternally.

Happy Halloween,
Old Sport!
Thus far time has kept us between
your knees, bound to disport
ourselves to your satisfaction
until the ultimate contraction
of your molten prostate heaves the spasm
that will wash us down the Chasm.

LOOKING DOWN

for Ron Overton

1

Beneath the street
they say
the ancient railway tunnel
still burrows
toward the harbor,
the crypt
of fine brick arches
forever sealed at either end,
the last locomotive
of the canceled line
stalled mid-tunnel,
fallen forward, crouching
like a maimed animal
on its shattered forewheels,
the fantastic
bell-shaped smokestack
thinned down by rust
to the crisp fragility
of fine porcelain,
the boiler alive
with nesting rats.
Cellars
deep beneath the street
conceal manholes
that open on
the sprawled abandon
of the rotting engine

and visceral roll
of the tunnel
into blackness.

2

In Greenwood Cemetery
the marble statue
of a recording angel
sits above
the hillside mausoleum,
covering, it seems,
a peephole
that penetrates
the double sarcophagus
of the Victorian couple
who lie, exposed,
below.
When the rather gripping
intimacy
of their mutual
decomposition
grew intense,
and the line
of titillated
observers lengthened
shamefully,
the prim officials

of the cemetery
moved in the angel
and had the peephole closed.

3

The last person
who saw Lincoln
remembered how
as a boy
he looked
down
into the small
window
at the coffin's head
and saw
the face,
its famous beard
miraculously alive
and glittering
with stars
of silver mold,
before concrete,
the ultimate protection
against graverobbers,
was poured in
to shut
the image
off.

4

Mathew Brady
knew the awful beauty
of the dead
and proved it,
fixing them
as they lay
on the battlefield
beneath
his probing camera,
mouths open, eyes deep,
skulls fusing
wonderfully
with their flesh,
legs wrenched open
to the sky,
fulfilling perfectly
his lust
and ours.

ALBUM

The big black bear
cuddled next to the hunter
in the white snow
is dead;
so are the bucks,
nestled like kittens
in the tall weeds,
their antlers dry as twigs;
so are the trout,
mouths hooked together
and displayed
against a well-grained
wood plank;
so is the black-haired
younger brother
who hitched up his pants
and balanced on a log raft
with the men from the mill;
so is his fine bay horse,
hitched to a trim little rig
and staring straight ahead
into the sepia field
where he was foaled
and later buried.

THE LAST OF
THE BOY KING,
EDWARD VI

Up through Greenwich park,
up through Greenwich park
to Blackheath,
the young king,
already dying,
rode up the hill
through Greenwich park
to Blackheath,
dressed in his favorite colors
of red and white and violet,
which made quite astonishing
his bright orange hair;
and his equerries
liveried in silver and green
made even more astonishing
Edward's red and white and violet,
his bright orange hair
and enamel-white skin.

I ate an apple tart
made with cinnamon
and coarse sugar
in Greenwich park
and walked up the hill
to Blackheath,
and there was plentiful

green grass
and schoolgirls
and an absence
of horses
and running.

The young king and his company
came up the hill to Blackheath
from the palace at Greenwich,
assembled on the plate-flat field
and ran at rings with their lances,
Edward's red and white and violet,
the silver and green equerries,
the lords and knights,
all charged at the rings with their lances,
filling the heath with rushing
and cries.

I came up the hill to Blackheath,
and two dozen vans and lorries
were stopped on the heath
so their drivers could piss out
their afternoon quota of bitter
before heading south.
And there was an absence of horses
and running,
of red and of white and of violet,
of silver and green,

but the heath still lay
flat as a plate
offered up to the wind.

Shortly before his death,
Edward, too weak to go out,
stood in his window
at Greenwich,
red and white and violet
and orange,
and saw the fleet
pass in review
on the narrow gray river
and heard the salute
of his ordnance
and the enormous
silence that followed.

CLIPPER SHIP

Do you feel the speed of it?
Do you hear
the hum of this dreadful,
beautiful hull hissing
through the water?
The delicate bowsprit,
poised exquisitely,
is deadly
as a hawk's beak,
as knife-slit focused
as his eye.
We lie in our hammocks
slung from the perfect
cage of wooden ribs
and cause the terror
and make the gasp of speed
to happen.
Remember, remember,
remember,
we say to ourselves,
the veined, clotted hand,
the ferocious, tender lines
of the groin,
remember, remember
the taste of salt,
the taste of blood.
We burst from our hammocks,
roaring out of our husks
and into the rigging.

The spider's web
of lines between us
cracks into place,
as taut as steel,
as dry as fire.
The royals, the topgallants,
the skysails
belly out,
and the fathoms
of black-green water
beneath us
are sliced open
by the endless speed
of the hull.

THERE   AND THERE

There—
at the soft place
behind the ear,
close to the hair,
where it is warm,
stung by the metal
tongue,
the neck
is lashed off
tight
by the black calf
leather.
They asked how
he managed to bring
his belt with him
into the cell.
There will be
an investigation
about bringing belts
into the cells.
And there—
the young blue arteries
feeding the groin
choked
at the impact;
the shriek
of his manhood
startled, falsetto,
then clotted
to silence.

FAMILY FUNERAL

At twelve I went to sleep
with your face,
a dream mask,
pressed to my face;
the weight,
I could have, would have sworn,
of your mouth
resting on my mouth;
your heavy hair
thick
between my sleep-padded
fingers.

Now I find you again,
risen
from beside your mother's grave,
come away with her hair,
her face,
buried deep inside
her insulated woman's body.

We touch carefully,
standing in the iced,
raw clay;
your voice has changed
to her voice
and yet remains
enough your own
to bring the sleeping

love-sick child in me
to tears and hopeless
fear of waking.

THE WHITE DREAM

for Mary Reid Chambers

1

She drew heads of Christ
for people she knew,
her living room
frequently lined with them,
all of the heads
looking, it seemed, much
alike.
She drew them neatly,
flat, almost Byzantine,
in oil on canvas,
filling in areas
of color
she thought appropriate
to Palestine—
brown and beige,
yellow, off-white
(the Christs inevitably
having healthy tans).
But she knew
some ancient tricks,
too,
and there was something
in the oversize
simplified
eyes,
and gentle mouths,
trapped between mustaches

and beards,
that made the heads
quite different
one from another,
within the formula.
"You won't understand yours,"
she said to me,
"for at least
twenty years."

2

I had the white dream
again last night,
the reconciliation dream
I call it,
and it was worse
than it had ever
been before
because it had become
pure white,
all color
drained away.
and it had gone
beyond hope.
beyond desire,
to become, in fact,
pure need

bleached white.
We sat side by side,
my brother
my twin and I,
nearly touching
but not,
the need
to come together
become a filtered
scream,
white sound.
And I knew
I would always
want him
and nothing else
and settle
for nothing else.

3

She was very nervous,
tormented,
flew into rages
after painting her Christs,
complaining that even
after tranquilizers
her limbs would jerk
uncontrollably when she

lay down
in her bed.
Nevertheless,
she went on
capturing our souls
in those eyes
and mouths,
taking us as far
ahead
into our lives
as sheer will
and the hard
bunched fist
of celibacy
would allow.
I've kept
my picture
at the back
of my closet,
turned to the wall
for almost twenty years.
I know
without looking
what I'd see
if I looked.

BROOKLYN—1900 AND AFTER

Just after dawn
I ride down to the docks
on the back of a cart,
down into the morning fog,
the town receding,
and I am swallowed up by the river,
the smell of it come around me from behind,
carried on the fog.
I float free,
my life in the hands of the driver
who holds the reins bunched in his fist.
The cobbled street falls away into the cleft
   of the hill
and I dangle my feet over nothing;
the horses' hooves
drop one by one into the chasm.
The voices of the stevedores
bob up to me like bits of meat in soup.
When the winch chains shriek, the fog lifts
and I jump off the cart,
dodging men and horses,
kicking manure, mixing it into the light snow
with the rest of them.

At night when I've eaten
I go to the church social hall
to set up chairs for the men;
I place spittoons in the four corners of the
   room

and I light the naked gas jets on the walls.
The boxers from Red Hook
burn in the light,
their hard bodies, oiled with sweat and blood,
smell sharp red in the heat.
I hold a fighter's knotted belly
while he pukes his teeth into a galvanized pail.
When I've cleaned up the hall
I go to the boarding house, blood still caught
in crimson halfmoons under my nails.

They began to die at home;
the gray wood house in Jersey is cold,
so I kept the stoves burning
and carried their tepid slopjars
across the yard to the outhouse.
After each of them died,
I stripped the bed and threw out the sheets;
the filth of death lingers,
even after carbolic and ammonia.
Then it was too late to go back to Brooklyn;
the horsecarts were gone from the docks
and the streets to the river were hacked off,
a highway burned across their stumps.
So I am alone here
because they all died.

I've looked you in the face
at last, my love.
Every petal
of the cut rose
has opened full,
and red is red,
beyond, beyond.
I've seen you now
quite clearly;
the icon's
bleeding mouth
and crusted eyes
are round
black holes
in the dull gold
paint.
I've looked at you
straight on,
my love,
and touched
your torn face
and whisper-soft
slit tongue.
I know you now,
my love;
your need is
stitched
into the soft
white pod

of your skin.
I know the fire,
my love,
and bring it
to you,
licking
from my fingertips.

FULTON STREET FERRY PIER

Brooklyn

The stones are here—
a few timbers
and rusted bolts
are all that's left
of the ferry pier.
But the stone fill
that held it up,
that was packed
around the wood pilings,
that held up the sheds,
that held up the towers and gables,
those stones are here.
Most of the stones
turn black at high tide
(slick with weeds,
oily with salt);
some are dry
and bleached gray
at low tide;
other stones
remain beneath
and are always
dark and wet.
Above,
the huge, impossible
flight of the bridge
fills the sky
as it soars
beyond its stones,

beyond all mass,
with the piercing,
needle-sharp
cry
of release
from what passed
for reason.

BRINGING IT IN

". . . it is believed that traffickers used the bodies and caskets of American servicemen to smuggle drugs into the U.S. from Southeast Asia." Time, *January 1, 1973.*

They're bringing it in
in corpses,
tucking it into
suitable cavities
and orifices,
poking it up,
suturing it in
snugly,
neat as Bull Durham
in drawstring pouches.
They're clever and tidy
about bringing it in,
keeping the country
consistently higher
by stuffing
securely
postadolescent
colons and tracts
with more opulent pleasure
than they could have
commanded
in life.

61

MEMORIAL DAY

for Leonard Felder

Go in and out the window
go in and out the window
go in and out the window
as you have done before:
now the *Normandie* is turning,
swung around by the harbor pilot,
turning from a fixed point,
a stately minute hand
pointing toward me slowly,
shaving across the eyes of my binoculars.
The sun is red when I look up,
brought together by my eyes
to the place where the glasses hinge,
and it is round as an apple
filling my mouth.
I play the game we played
as I go in and out the window,
and time ticks as it has ticked before,
not more slowly, but more;
and the ship does not dock
down river but continues to turn
in that direction, as it has turned before.

I hurt. The doctor says he knows,
but he does not—did not—know
how pain is carried along
(pass it along)
by the cars going down the Drive,
by the yellow cabs, by the Hudsons,

by the long LaSalles,
each one carrying a piece of it
as they have done before.
But they can never take it all away;
for the pain goes in and out
the window through my eyes,
in their long, black
simulated-leather tubes.
Today, if it is today,
they celebrated at the salt-shaker
monument to dead soldiers and sailors.
I saw it with my glasses:
the flags and the flower wreaths
and how the honor guard laughed,
winking at each other
(my glasses are strong),
and how one of the sailors
in the navy band
had three of his thirteen buttons
undone but didn't dare look down.
They played "Columbia, the Gem of
    the Ocean,"
which I play on my Victrola
when I am able to wind it up,
holding the black wood knob in my palm.

I go in and out the window;
my eyes help me do it
(my legs hurt too much).

I go in and out the window—
but no further. I am not scared
when I look into the room
and see, reflected in my picture
of a caravel under full sail,
the reflection of the window
and of my going out,
because it does not change or stop anything,
I have done it all before,
and the cars go down the Drive,
bearing away pieces of my pain
as they have done before
(although there is always more
for them to take away,
it matters less);
the *Normandie* always turns
but never docks,
ticking in toward shore
as it has done before;
and the sailor,
afraid to look down,
still plays his horn.

I go in and out the window when the sun
flicks my glasses with its red tongue.
I see the points and pinnacles,
I see the sharp iron fence
and scratchy shrubbery
of the Schwab house

(my private castle)
as I have seen it before.
But I see more,
as I have done before
when I have gone out the window
with my long black eyes.
Each spire and pinnacle
of my castle, each spike
of the iron fence, each pointed
branch of shrubbery
spears, skewers a bit of my curdled
    red pain;
my whole castle
is alive with it.
It does not go away,
but stays, as it has done before.

And the doctor does things
as he has done before,
but it is the same because
he must always go into the next room
and I must always remain here
at my window, searching out,
when night comes, the lights
on the Palisades
as they twine and weave,
as they climb the electric mountain
of the rollercoaster
and are thrown down, shrieking.

And I run with them for awhile,
snaking inside the long, thin,
hissing strings of light,
moving fast, so fast
that I—not forget, not lose—
but run along the outer rim
of my pain,
come out my window for awhile
before it catches me again.

I no longer remember,
as you can plainly see,
exactly how we played the game.
You hear me chant the rhyme
as I go in and out the window
in and out the window
as I have done before.
I think we caught each other,
brought our ring of arms down
as someone wove in and out,
but I'm not sure now.
I hear the children in the park
sing the rhyme
but they do not really know
the game—not even as well as I.
For I know it doesn't stop.
I heard the chant still and saw
the window—even when the doctor
pulled down the sheet,

looked at my chest,
my stomach,
my thing
(between its apricot mounds)
and then pulled the sheet up
over my face.

Nothing stops:
the *Normandie* moves toward shore;
the Hudsons and LaSalles
go one by one, line by line
down the Drive, under the trees,
as they have done before;
the sailor plays on
(ignoring what time in the button factory
it is or ever was).
The fence around the Schwab house
contains, surrounds;
the river is reflected in the picture
on my wall;
the doctor has gone into the other room
and I remain, looking out and in
with my black binoculars,
adjusting the focus of my pain
with the ribbed black wheel in the center
as I go in and out the window
as I go in and out the window
as I go in and out the window
as I have done before.